DISNEY

Beaut
and the Beast

AUTUMN PUBLISHING

AUTUMN
PUBLISHING

Published in 2024
First published in the UK by Autumn Publishing
An imprint of Igloo Books Ltd
Cottage Farm, NN6 0BJ, UK
Owned by Bonnier Books
Sveavägen 56, Stockholm, Sweden
www.igloobooks.com

0424 001
2 4 6 8 10 9 7 5 3 1
ISBN 978-1-83795-920-4

Cover designed by Stephen Jorgensen

Printed and manufactured in China

This book
belongs to:

_____

Disney
Beauty and the Beast

I AM BELLE

I AM
BELLE.

I live in a small house
in a small town.

This is my father, MAURICE.

He's an INVENTOR.

Some of his inventions look a
little strange. I love that Papa sees
things in ways that others don't.

Living in our town is nice, but every day is exactly the same.

I FEED THE ANIMALS...

... TEND THE GARDENS,

AND SHOP AT
THE MARKETS.

My favourite place to go is
the village bookshop.

I LOVE TO READ!

I've read everything in the bookstore –
some more than once.

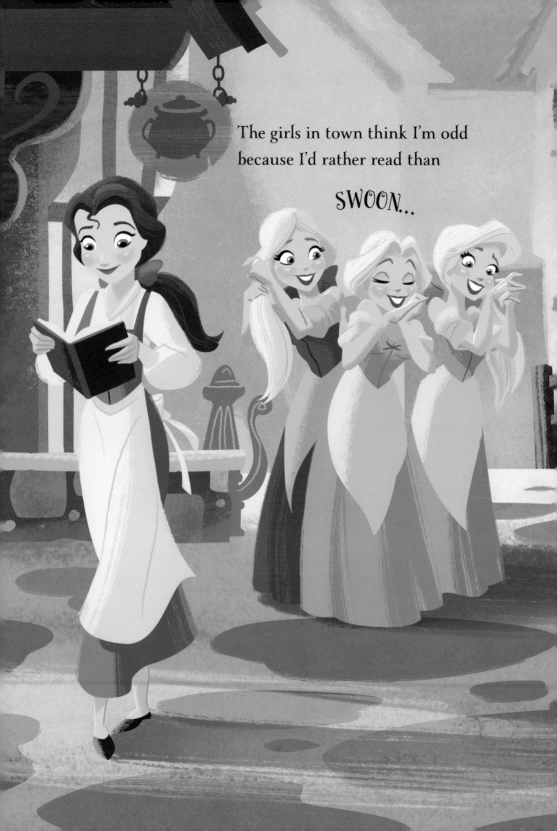

The girls in town think I'm odd because I'd rather read than

SWOON...

... over Gaston. They think he's so handsome. Gaston agrees!

I can be very BRAVE.
When my father went missing,
I raced into the woods and found
him locked up in a mysterious
castle by a creature called THE BEAST.
I offered to take my father's place as
the Beast's prisoner.

The castle was a strange and scary place filled with talking furniture! Luckily, I am good at making new friends.

I met a clock named Cogsworth, a candelabra named Lumiere, a teapot named Mrs. Potts and her son, Chip, a teacup.

I missed my father terribly and was in no mood to eat. But being served delicious food by singing and dancing silverware cheered me right up!

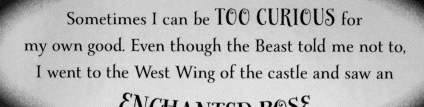

Sometimes I can be **TOO CURIOUS** for my own good. Even though the Beast told me not to, I went to the West Wing of the castle and saw an **ENCHANTED ROSE.**

I am comfortable around all creatures,
including little birds,

BIG horses...

... and even ENCHANTED
FOOTSTOOLS that act like DOGS.

CAN YOU GUESS which room in the Beast's castle I LIKE THE MOST?

I can bring out the best in people –
AND BEASTS. Once the Beast's
caring nature came out, he became
my favourite dance partner.

Thanks to the love I had for the Beast, the curse
that had been placed on everyone in his castle
was lifted! They all became human again.
That chapter of my life was more exciting
than any in my favourite books!

DISNEP
Beauty and the Beast

I AM THE BEAST

I AM THE BEAST.

I live in a **HUGE CASTLE** deep in the woods.

I have horns and claws, and I'm covered in fur.

I used to be
a human prince.
I had power and
riches, but I didn't
care about anyone
except myself.

I DON'T LIKE ROSES.

An old beggar once asked permission to stay in my castle in exchange for a rose. I laughed at her and told her to leave.

The woman was an
ENCHANTRESS IN DISGUISE!
As punishment for my lack of
kindness, she turned me
into a beast and put a
curse on all who lived in
my castle.

My loyal servants were transformed
into enchanted household objects.

LUMIERE became a candelabra.

COGSWORTH turned into a clock.

MRS. POTTS became a teapot.

And her son, CHIP, became a teacup.

The enchantress left a magical rose in
the West Wing of my castle.

If all the flower's
PETALS
FELL

before I learnt to love someone –
and won her love as well – we would
stay cursed forever.

I'm not a good
HOST.

The first visitor to my castle in years was a man named
MAURICE. I locked him in my dungeon.

His daughter, BELLE, arrived soon after. She was VERY BRAVE, and convinced me to let her father go. She promised to take his place as my prisoner.

I have a bit of a **TEMPER**. When I caught Belle trespassing in the West Wing, I was scared she was going to touch the rose.

I **YELLED** so loudly, she ran right out of the castle.

I am **BIG** and **STRONG**,

but fighting off a pack of wolves wasn't easy.

I can be

CRANKY

when I'm hurt. Belle was patient
as she cleaned my wounds.

Small animals used to be afraid
of me. Belle taught me how to be
gentle and kind.

You might think I have bad table manners...

... but it's hard to hold a spoon with these giant, furry beast hands!

I don't look graceful. Turns out I'm a good dancer – with the right partner!

Falling in love with Belle was easy, but I never expected her to love me in return. She is a special person. She saw past my hideous exterior.

Thanks to Belle's love, the curse was lifted.

I AM THE BEAST NO MORE.